The Smurf's Apprentice

Random House 🏠 New York

This adaptation copyright © 1982 by Peyo. License of SEPP Brussels. All rights reserved under International and Pan-American Copyright Conventions. Published in the United States by Random House, Inc., New York, and simultaneously in Canada by Random House of Canada Limited, Toronto. Based on original story by Peyo. Published in different form by Hodder & Stoughton Ltd., London. Copyright © 1975 Peyo and SEPP Brussels. English text copyright © 1979 Hodder & Stoughton Ltd. Library of Congress Catalog Card Number: 81-85942   ISBN: 0-394-85373-3 Manufactured in the United States of America   1 2 3 4 5 6 7 8 9 0 SMURF is a trademark of SEPP International S.A.

Papa Smurf knew a lot about magic. He experimented in his laboratory at night when the other Smurfs were asleep.

But one night Little Smurf went and peeked into Papa Smurf's window.

The next day Little Smurf said, "Papa Smurf, I'd like to be your apprentice! I think I've got a real gift for magic."

"You're much too young," said Papa Smurf. "We'll talk about it when you're older."

Little Smurf was mad. "I'll show him," he muttered.

"I'll never smurf any magic at this rate," sighed Little Smurf. Then he thought of something. "Our enemy, Gargamel, is a wizard! He must have a book of magic spells!"

So Little Smurf made his way through the forest to Gargamel's house.

Little Smurf slipped into the wizard's house. No one was home. The book of spells was too heavy to carry, so the Smurf tore out a page.

Then he heard Gargamel coming. The Smurf quickly slipped out and ran home.

But Little Smurf had a problem. Only part of the spell was on the page. The rest was on the next page ... and that page was still in Gargamel's book!

"I don't even know what this spell is for," said Little Smurf, worried.

But that didn't stop him. He gathered the ingredients and mixed them together.

Glug, glug, glug went the potion down Little Smurf's throat. And something very strange happened!

"Oh no!" gasped the Smurf as he looked at himself. "My skin is green and scaly! And I have an enormous tail! What will I do now?"

None of the other Smurfs knew what to do about Little Smurf either. Papa Smurf gave him pills and potions, but nothing worked. Little Smurf was still green and scaly.

"That's what comes of not listening to me," said Papa Smurf to Little Smurf.

Little Smurf was very sad. The next day he wrote a note and pinned it to his door.

"I've gone to Gargamel's place to find a cure for this spell. Love, Smurf."

Then he set off through the woods.

This time Gargamel was waiting for Little Smurf and had a trap ready.

As Little Smurf climbed up to the book of spells a cage fell over him. He shook in fear as Gargamel came out of hiding.

"Ha, ha!" cackled the wicked wizard. "I've finally caught you! Now to experiment on my ugly little spell stealer!"

Suddenly there was shouting!

"Leave that Smurf alone, Gargamel . . . or you'll be sorry!" yelled Papa and the other Smurfs at the window.

Then they jumped down into the room.

"I'll get all of you this time!" cried Gargamel as he chased the Smurfs around.

Some Smurfs climbed onto the shelf. Others tripped Gargamel. He crashed to the floor.

Then the Smurfs on the shelf tipped a big pot of sticky glue over him.

"Oh, you rotten little Smurfs!" screamed Gargamel. "I'll get you yet!"

But try as he did, Gargamel was stuck to the floor.

"Here's the cure," said Papa Smurf as he looked through the wizard's book. "Let's get it ready before Gargamel becomes unstuck!"

The Smurfs all helped, and soon the mixture was ready.

Glug, glug, glug it went down Little Smurf's throat.

Instantly his green skin and long tail disappeared. He was his smurfy blue self again! And just in time, too—for Gargamel began to move!

"Hooray! The cure worked! Now let's get out of here," Papa Smurf said.

"Foiled again!" sobbed Gargamel as his little enemies ran away into the woods. "It's not fair! I'm big and strong, and they're small and weak! But I never win!"